KATIE WOO
and PEDRO
Mysteries

The Rainbow Mystery

by Fran Manushkin

illustrated by Tammie Lyon

WITHDRAWN

PICTURE WINDOW BOOKS
a capstone imprint

Published by Picture Window Books, an imprint of Capstone
1710 Roe Crest Drive, North Mankato, Minnesota 56003
capstonepub.com

Text copyright © 2022 by Fran Manushkin
Illustrations copyright © 2022 by Capstone

Library of Congress Cataloging-in-Publication Data
Names: Manushkin, Fran, author. | Lyon, Tammie, illustrator.
Title: The rainbow mystery / by Fran Manushkin ; illustrated by Tammie Lyon.
Description: North Mankato, Minnesota : Picture Window Books, an imprint of Capstone, [2022] | Series: Katie Woo and Pedro mysteries | Audience: Ages 5–7 | Audience: Grades K–1 | Summary: When Katie's father loses his special rainbow ring while playing with the kids in the backyard, Katie and Pedro work to follow the clues to find the missing ring.
Identifiers: LCCN 2021029981 (print) | LCCN 2021029982 (ebook) | ISBN 9781663958662 (hardcover) | ISBN 9781666332162 (paperback) | ISBN 9781666332179 (pdf)
Subjects: LCSH: Woo, Katie (Fictitious character)—Juvenile fiction. | Chinese Americans—Juvenile fiction. | Hispanic Americans—Juvenile fiction. | Lost articles—Juvenile fiction. | Fathers and daughters—Juvenile fiction. | CYAC: Mystery and detective stories. | Lost and found possessions—Fiction. | Fathers and daughters—Fiction. | Chinese Americans—Fiction. | Hispanic Americans—Fiction. | LCGFT: Detective and mystery fiction. | Picture books.
Classification: LCC PZ7.M3195 Rai 2022 (print) | LCC PZ7.M3195 (ebook) | DDC 813.54 [E]—dc23
LC record available at https://lccn.loc.gov/2021029981
LC ebook record available at https://lccn.loc.gov/2021029982

Design Elements by Shutterstock: Darcraft, Magnia
Designed by Dina Her

Printed and bound in the USA. PO4608

Table of Contents

Chapter 1

A Spring Day

It was springtime. The sun
was shining, and the birds
were singing.

Katie said, "Let's play ball!"

"Great idea," said her dad.

His new ring sparkled in

the sunlight.

"Your ring is so cool,"

said Katie. "It shines like a

rainbow. But it looks a little

loose."

"It is," said Katie's dad.

"I should get it fixed."

Katie tossed him the ball.

"*Squawk!*" The ball almost

hit a blue jay.

"Oops!" said Katie.

"Sorry!"

Later, Pedro came over.

They played in the tall grass.

When they got hungry,

Katie's dad made hot dogs.

"Uh-oh." Katie pointed

to his finger. "Where is your

ring?"

"It's gone!" said Katie's dad.
"We have to find it. Mom gave
it to me for my birthday."

But—*BOOM!* A big storm
began. They had to run inside.

Chapter 2

Searching for Treasure

Finally, the storm was over.

"Look!" Katie shouted.

"There's a rainbow. The end of

the rainbow leads to treasure."

"Cool!" said Pedro.

"Come on," said Katie's dad. "The treasure I want to find is my ring."

He began looking in the bushes and the grass.

Whoosh! A bird flew by.

"There are lots of blue jays today," said Katie. "See the grass in her beak? She is making a nest."

"Forget the blue jays,

and let's find the missing

ring," said Pedro. "I am

great at solving mysteries.

Let's look for a clue."

Katie's dog began digging

in the grass.

"That's a clue!" yelled

Pedro. "Koko smells the ring!"

No! It was a bone.

The rainbow was still shining.

"That rainbow has to bring us luck," said Katie. "It *has* to."

But Katie's father looked sadder and sadder.

Katie sat down on her
swing.

"Why are you playing?"
asked Pedro. "We have to
find your dad's ring."

"Swinging helps me think,"

said Katie.

Plop! A nut fell on her head.

"Silly blue jay!" she yelled.

"You dropped your food."

But it made her think.

Chapter 3

Mystery Solved!

Katie began swinging

higher—and higher! Soon she

could see the top of the tree.

"What do you see?" asked

Pedro.

"I see a squirrel chasing another squirrel," said Katie.

"That's fun," said Pedro.

"But it does not help us find the ring."

But Katie kept looking.

"Dad!" she yelled. "I see
something shiny up there.
I think it's your ring."

"No way," said her dad.
"Rings can't fly."

"I know!" said Katie.
"But birds can. They like
taking shiny things for their
nests. Dad, can you
climb the tree?"

"For sure!" said her dad.

He climbed to the top.

"*Squawk!*" cried the blue jay.

"Yay!" yelled Katie's dad.

"My ring was in her nest!"

He waved the ring high.

"Look!" shouted Katie.

"This tree is at the end of the

rainbow. The treasure is your

ring!"

"*You* are the treasure,"
said Katie's dad, hugging
her.

"And a great detective,"
said Pedro.

About the Author

Fran Manushkin is the author of Katie Woo, the highly acclaimed fan-favorite early-reader series, as well as the popular Pedro series. Her other books include *Happy in Our Skin*, *Plenty of Hugs!*, *Baby, Come Out!*, and the best-selling board books *Big Girl Panties* and *Big Boy Underpants*. There is a real Katie Woo: Fran's great-niece, but she doesn't get into as much trouble as the Katie in the books. Fran lives in New York City, three blocks from Central Park, where she can often be found bird-watching and daydreaming. She writes at her dining room table, without the help of her naughty cats, Goldy and Chaim.

About the Illustrator

Tammie Lyon, the illustrator of the Katie Woo and Pedro series, says that these characters are two of her favorites. Tammie has illustrated work for Disney, Scholastic, Simon and Schuster, Penguin, HarperCollins, and Amazon Publishing, to name a few. She is also an author/illustrator of her own stories. Her first picture book, *Olive and Snowflake*, was released to starred reviews from *Kirkus* and *School Library Journal*. Tammie lives in Cincinnati, Ohio, with her husband Lee and two dogs, Amos and Artie. She spends her days working in her home studio in the woods, surrounded by wildlife and, of course, two mostly-always-sleeping dogs.

Glossary

clue (KLOO)—something that helps someone find something or solve a mystery

detective (dee-TEK-tiv)—a person who works to solve mysteries

mystery (MISS-tur-ee)—a puzzle or crime that needs to be solved

sparkle (SPAR-kuhl)—to give off small flashes of light

squirrel (SKWIR-uhl)—a small animal with a bushy tail

treasure (TREZH-er)—something that is highly valued

All About Mysteries

A mystery is a story where the main characters must figure out a puzzle or solve a crime. Let's think about *The Rainbow Mystery*.

Plot

In a mystery, the plot focuses on solving a problem. What is the problem in this story?

Clues

To solve a mystery, readers should look for clues. What are some of the clues in this mystery?

Red Herrings

Red herrings are bad clues. They do not help solve the mystery. Sometimes they even make the mystery harder to solve. What clues in this story were red herrings?

Thinking About the Story

1. Who solved the mystery of the missing ring? Did he or she have help? Who or what helped the detective?

2. Katie says that the rainbow has to bring her, Pedro, and her dad luck as they search for the ring. Do you think the rainbow did bring them luck?

3. What treasure would you like to find at the end of a rainbow? Draw a picture of a rainbow with your treasure at the end, and write a sentence to describe it.

A Walking
Water Rainbow

A rainbow helps Katie solve the mystery of her dad's missing ring. This rainbow project might not help you solve mysteries or lead to any treasure, but it's fun to do!

What you need:

- 6 identical pint-sized jars

- water

- blue, red, and yellow food coloring

- 6 paper towels

What you do:

1. Fill three jars with water. Then add blue food coloring to one jar, red to another, and yellow to the third.

2. Place all the jars in a circle in this order: red, empty jar, yellow, empty jar, blue, empty jar. The last empty jar should sit next the red jar.

3. Roll each paper towel into a tube. Put one end of the towel into a full jar and the other end into the empty jar next to it. Each jar will have two towel ends stuck inside it.

4. Now wait for your rainbow to form. While it will start right away, the process will take one to two days to complete. Have fun watching as the water moves and the rainbow grows!

Solve more mysteries with Katie and Pedro!

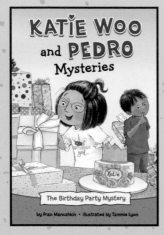

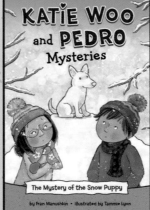